Katie-Bug Hugs

By Cathy Keevill

Illustrated by Veronica Chapman

This one is dedicated to my adorable Granddaughter Fiona Kate (AKA Katie-Bug). Love you sweet baby girl.

This is the story of a little girl named Katie-Bug.

Katie was average, like you and me.

She tumbled around and skinned her knee.

Her Mom was the queen and her Dad
was the king.
Katie was princess and
played on the swing.

Katie had books and games
and many fun toys.

She liked to be happy,
she liked to make noise.

She smiled and she laughed
and she loved to talk.

**On sunny, warm days
she took Speedy for a walk.**

Her friends would come over
to visit each day.

She learned very quickly to share
and to play.

She loved eating sandwiches,
veggies and fruits.

And stomping in puddles
in cute rubber boots.

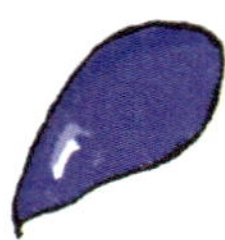

She sat in the mud with a
really big splash.

Then Mama said,
"Katie! You need a bath!"

Dad filled the tub with
water and bubbles.
Katie climbed in
without any troubles.

The water got cold. She had chills down her back.

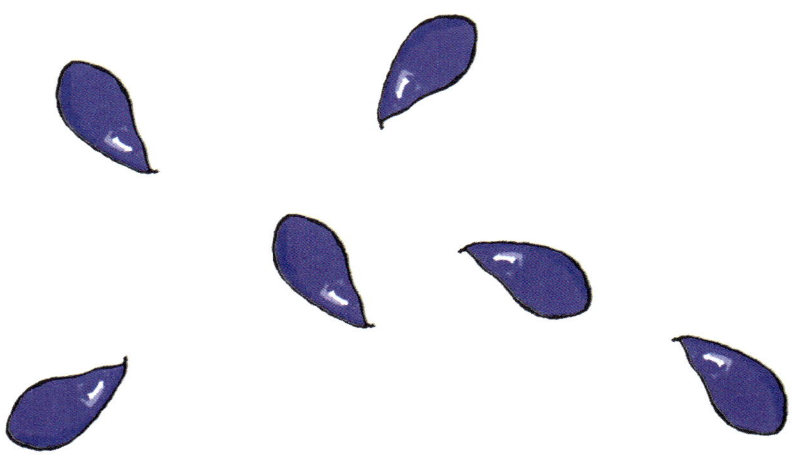

She had to get out for her
bedtime snack.

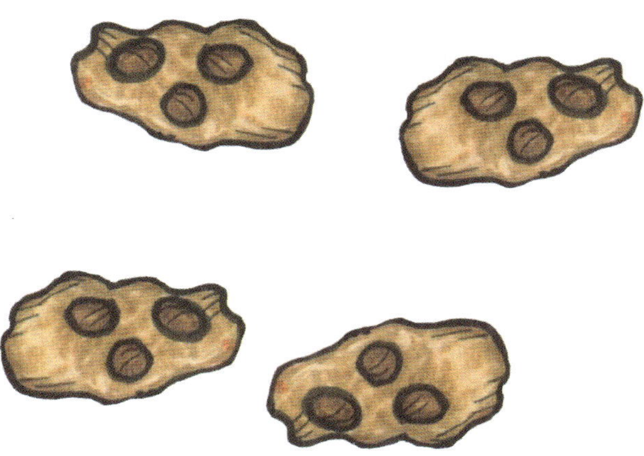

Her Mama said
"Katie it's time for bed."
Katie said "No,"
and then shook her head.

Mama-Bug frowned and
called Katie's Dad.
But Katie-Bug giggled,
that made her glad.

Daddy would cuddle and read her a book.
Under the bed for monsters he'd look.

**When it is safe and
the monsters all gone, Daddy kisses
Katie and sings her their song.**

♫
Katie-Bug darling. Katie it's time.
The day is all over, wee Katie of mine.
Cuddled and snuggled and stories all read.
Katie my darling climb into bed.
Snuggle in warm and snuggle down tight.
Katie I love you, now say good night. ♫

Her parents tuck little Katie all snug
and just right.
They kiss her nose and tell her good-
night.

Then Mama and Daddy give her nose
a small tug.
Because nothing's as sweet as a
Katie-Bug hug.

Good night and sweet dreams.

Can you Find?

Speedy sleeping.
Ten lady bugs.
Katie's dad.
Katie-Bug sleeping.
Kids playing jump rope.
A king.
A swing.
A book.
A queen.
A pillow.
A lady bug back pack.
Lady bug antennas.
Four water drops.
A rubber ducky.
Cookies.
The moon.
Katie-Bug's mom.
A laundry hamper.

Special thanks to Veronica
for her hard work and
excellent illustrations.

Made in the USA
Columbia, SC
19 May 2018